The
Night Thief

One bright night when the moon was high, the Night Thief crept into town. He waited until the city was dark and everyone was fast asleep—everyone except Nedra. She sat in her little room at the top of the house, looking out the window, wishing upon a star.

Nedra watched as the Night Thief, in a burglar mask, pulled out a big black bag. He tossed his magic rope high into the sky and lassoed the moon. Then the Night Thief pulled and pulled the big yellow moon from the sky and tucked it carefully into his sack.

Next, he plucked each twinkling star, big and small, from the sky and sprinkled them into his bag. The last thing he did was grab the edge of the night sky and he rolled it and rolled it up until it fit just right next to the moon and stars in his sack. Then the Night Thief crept away, leaving the sun shining brightly in the sky.

It had all happened so quickly, Nedra could hardly believe she had really seen the Night Thief steal the night. The sudden sunlight woke up the whole town.

"What happened to the night?" everyone was asking.

"The Night Thief stole it!" Nedra cried. But no one would listen.

Everyone talked excitedly. "How will we sleep without the night?" someone said.

"How will we know when it's time to sleep?" someone else asked.

"But what happened to the night?" they all wondered.

Nobody would listen to Nedra so she finally went to see her grandfather.

"Grandfather, last night I saw the Night Thief steal the night. He put everything in a big black bag and disappeared."

Grandfather sat down and lit his pipe. "You know, when I was a little boy just your age, something like this happened. One night I couldn't sleep and I was looking out the window, and suddenly I saw a man in a burglar mask."

"The Night Thief!" Nedra cried.

Grandfather nodded his head. "He was sneaking around stuffing stars into a big black bag."

"What did you do?"

"Well, I opened my window and yelled at him to put back the night. And then I ran to get my parents. But when I got back, the Night Thief had disappeared. I guess I caught him just in time, because we didn't lose the night."

"I should have stopped him," Nedra said sadly. "Now the night is gone and it's all my fault."

Grandfather gave her a hug. "Not if you find the Night Thief and bring back the night."

"How can I do that?"

"You've got to look for clues," Grandfather said. "Maybe he dropped something or left something behind."

So Nedra searched for clues. She looked in the park and in the school yard. She searched the playground, underneath

Finally, Nedra was tired and she wandered down to the river. "I'll never be able to find the Night Thief," she said sadly. She sat down on a rock and began to cry.

Just then, Nedra saw something sparkling in the grass. She picked it up. It was a little star! In fact, there were lots of stars, all twinkling blue and gold and green and yellow in the sunlight.

"The Night Thief must have dropped these! He must have had a hole in his bag!" Nedra exclaimed as she followed the sparkling trail. She picked her way along the road, following the little ribbon of stars past thick green forests and broken old houses until she came at last to a dark and lonely cave. It was so big and so dark that it reminded Nedra of a giant opening his mouth.

The twinkling path of stars led inside the cave and lit up the darkness. Nedra shivered when she saw furry black bats hanging from the ceiling.

She began to be afraid. This cave was very dark and scary. Nedra had just decided to turn around and go home, when she saw a bright light at the very far end of a tunnel. And a ribbon of stars lit the way! So Nedra tiptoed down the rocky tunnel toward the light.

She finally reached the end of the tunnel and there to her surprise hung the moon, gold and sparkling in the darkness! The little stars danced in the moonlight. "So this is where the Night Thief hid the night!" Nedra whispered.

Suddenly, wild laughter echoed through the cave and Nedra looked up to the top of a cliff. There sat the Night Thief in a crystal chair. He was hunched over, counting the stars and laughing.

"Two thousand one hundred and seven, two thousand one hundred and eight." He laughed again. "Now I'm the only one who will ever see the night! For everyone else, the night is now gone forever!"

He smiled and counted the stars. As he counted each little star, he plucked it from the darkness and dropped it into the black bag at his feet. Soon, he tired of counting and fell asleep.

Nedra stood quietly in the shadows until she heard the Night Thief snore. She had to get that bag! Nedra was really afraid now, but she climbed silently step by step along the rocky edge. As Nedra reached the top of the cliff, she tiptoed up behind the Night Thief and quietly picked up the bagful of stars. Nedra dropped the bag to the bottom of the cliff where it landed with a loud THUMP!

The noise woke the Night Thief and he jumped up from his chair. "Who are you? What have you done with my stars?" he demanded.

Standing on the edge of the cliff, Nedra slipped and fell.
"Help me!" she cried as she fell. She could hear the Night
Thief's evil laughter. The golden moon glistened in the cold
darkness above Nedra's head, just waiting to be caught.
Nedra caught hold of the moon and floated gently down,
down, down to the ground.

She sat on the ground catching her breath, when Nedra heard the Night Thief climbing slowly down the rocky cliff. Nedra quickly pushed the moon into the bag and gathered up as many stars as she could. Then she pulled the black sky down, rolling it up carefully so that it wouldn't tear. She could hear the Night Thief climbing step by step down the cliff. "Give me back my stars!" he yelled.

Nedra began to run, the heavy bag thumping against her legs. The sleepy bats shifted uneasily as Nedra carried the black bag out of the tunnel and into the daylight.

Nedra was in such a hurry that she tripped on a rock and fell. The bag flew out of her hands and the dark sky tumbled out. It rolled down the hill, faster and faster, darkening the sunny sky as it went. The stars had spilled on the ground in a shimmering pile of light.

Nedra could hear the howls of the Night Thief echoing angrily through the cave. She had to hurry and put back the night! Nedra gently touched the sparkling stars. They gave off a soft warm glow and Nedra wished she could take them home.

Suddenly, the bats fluttered out of the cave looking for food. WHOOSH! Their flapping wings swept the stars high into the velvet sky until it twinkled with silver.

"Give me back the night! It's mine!" shouted the Night Thief as he stood at the mouth of the cave.

He screamed so loudly and so angrily that the stones from the ceiling began to fall. Huge rocks fell with a loud BOOM!

Nedra couldn't see the Night Thief anymore, but she could still hear him yelling inside the cave. The Night Thief wouldn't be back for a long time!

Nedra bounced the moon from star to star until it found its proper place in the sky. The golden light of the moon lit Nedra's way home.

When the townspeople saw that the night had returned, they all cheered and went back to bed. Nedra's grandfather looked out his window at the sparkling night sky and smiled.

And in her little room at the top of the house, Nedra slept soundly in her cozy bed, dreaming wonderful nighttime dreams.